ALWAYS BY OUR SIDE

MITCHELL'S STORY

(A foster puppy's account of his first year preparing to be a future dog guide. He taught his foster family everything they needed to know about life!)

By Susan Kerr

Copyright 2013 by Susan Kerr

Published by Sarah Book Publishing
(A subsidiary of Litewill Holdings, LLC)
www.sarahbookpublishing.com

85 Industrial Drive Brownsville, TX 78521

ISBN: 978-1-61456-146-0

First Edition: April 2014

Book Cover Design: Digital Print Shoppe

www.digiprintshoppe.com

Printed in the United States of America

PROLOGUE

Labradors, Golden Retrievers, Poodles of all sizes, Jack Russell Terriers, and Border Terrier puppies destined to become dog guides with the Lions Foundation (www. dogguides.com) are sometimes donated by approved dog breeders, but usually are born in Lions Foundation puppy facility in Breslau, Ontario, Canada. That is a jolly, happy place with staff and volunteers who get to play with the puppies early on in the puppies' lives to get them used to two-legged people. Puppies make friends quickly and it sure must be fun to be down on the floor with them when they start scrambling around exploring your fingers and toes! And licking your nose!

As soon as they are old enough to leave their moms, at about 6 or 7weeks of age, each pup is sent to a foster family for about a year to become really, really well mannered. All prepared and ready to go to Lions Foundation Doggie University in Oakville, Ontario, at about one year of age.

This is how Mitchell came to live with us. We went to pick him up and from the moment we met him we knew he was very special! And smart! We had never met a dog like him before! He is the only dog in the world who can write letters! So... we brought him home to St. Joseph Island to be our foster puppy for a year... and that's where our story begins...

FEBRUARY 1

Hi, Everyone!

My name is Mitchell... and I am a 14 week old Brown Standard Poodle.

Because I am already so clever I have been chosen for a special life. When I grow up I will be a dog guide for someone who does not see well, or perhaps does not hear well... or perhaps I will be an assistant to someone who needs a different kind of help. My job will be to live with them and be their very own always helper so they can enjoy life more. I am very happy about that!

But it is a bit scary because there is so much to learn before I start that important job! My lessons have started though, and I have come to live on St. Joseph Island with my new foster parents, Mommy Sue and Daddy Robert. They will help me learn lots of things.

Apparently, I can't just pee wherever and whenever I want. Who knew?

They have toys for me to play with and I have my own safe place for sleeping and hiding, called a crate. Mommy put a blanket over top so it is lovely and dark inside like a den... I have a cozy bed inside to sleep on and I am allowed to take a toy in there for company, because I miss my sisters and brothers very much, and am just learning to sleep by myself.

I did have a nice first mommy... I had a four-legged first mommy who fed me and licked me clean, and nuzzled me and sniffed me and nudged me to make me move over. She did the same things for my sisters and brothers. We always used to be trying to suckle her at once... and we climbed over each other for the best spot. She would just put her nose in among us and sort of pushed us around... we sure knew who the boss was!

First mommy....Can you see me? Huh? Huh?

I'm the one sitting up straight and tall!

PHOTOS COURTESY OF BIJOU POODLES

Then I had a second mommy... a two-legged one. She was especially nice! She would pick us up one by one and look at us... and at first, because our eyes were not open, we cried a little, because we could not see what was happening. But we soon learned that she was very gentle and was checking us out, making sure we were all Okay! Right away, when we first popped into the world, we felt her put something round our necks and later, when we were bigger we knew that they were our very first collars, made of soft stuff. We all had a different colour. Mine was Purple! I like that colour best.

She and some others like her would get on the floor with us, touch us all over, tickle our tummies and make us laugh. They were super friendly... some were big and some were little. Some we saw every day, others just once in a while. They made us feel very special. There were lots of these other mommies and daddies who sort of came and went and they only wanted to play with us. I loved them sooo much. They picked us up and cuddled us, and rolled us over to tickle our toes and tugged our ears and rubbed our feet. This was fun! When we could walk a little better they took us outside and we explored white stuff and tried to eat it. It was cold so we came in after a little while and ran after balls and played tug with squeaky toys. We chased each other too, my brothers and sisters, and I always won! After a playtime with these vol... volun... voluntrays or something, we were really tired and had good deep sleeps!

That's my dad watching over us while mom takes her turn at the beauty parlour. I am left of the baby lamb who snuck in... I am between two black brothers.

PHOTO COURTESY OF BIJOU POODLES

I grew so fast. I got bigger and stronger. I think it was all the good food from mommy. Then we were given this mushy stuff and we learned how to eat it by licking and slurping it out of a dish. I liked it. It was fun to put our feet in and slurp from the middle... my brothers and sisters were all trying to eat faster and more, so a guy had to get smart fast to get a fair share! We played a lot and I liked to roll around over top of the others, and we got to yipping a bit and nipping a bit and mommy would watch over us as we explored. Our big two-legged second mommy and all those other two-legged giants picked us up and cuddled us and made squeaky noises to us. They would hold us up and look in our eyes and snuffle us... it was nice because we could just about reach them with our tongues and then they squealed loud and laughed.

It is strange now not having my first mommy and my brother and sisters here with me... and sometimes I cry for them. My new foster mommy seems to know... and she picks me up and tells me everything is Okay. She has given me a teddy bear to cuddle with when I am in my little safe den. I am not scared of teddy bears.

I have my own dishes and a red collar and leash. I even have a special coat to wear when I am going for walks so you will know me when you see me. It says I am a Future Dog Guide.

So... hello to you... and I look forward to meeting you soon!

Yip! Yip!

Who is the cutest pup in the world?
Everyone says it's me!

PHOTOS COURTESY OF BIJOU POODLES

FEBRUARY 8

Hello... it's me, Mitchell!

Last time I wrote to you I had just arrived to live with my new foster parents. Already I feel right at home and I like my people. I can get them to do almost anything for me. I have learned that if I flip out my tongue... like *this*... and wiggle my bum... like *that*... I can get them to tickle me under my chin! Oh, what power I have!

They are a bit strange, though. Every time I wake up from a nap, and even in the middle of the night, they pick me up from my den and take me outside. They put me down in the snow and say "Hurry up, Mitch". I have no clue what they mean, so I ignore them and bury my head in the snow and hide. They keep saying "Hurry up, Mitch". Boooooring! So, I have invented a new game. I just pee in my nice smelly place in the yard... and then they do a silly dance and say "Good Boy, Mitch!" and tickle my ticklish spot on my back. Gee... I am so clever. I can make them do anything!

Someone new has been added to my life. I have my very own hairdresser person. At first, I was not very happy about being put into this big bathtub and getting a bubbly shampoo. The rubbing was nice, but then it rained on my face. I think I tried to run away, but this thing had me by the neck and I couldn't get away. Then, there was this noisy thing which blew hot air all over me and I tried to bite it... but after a while it felt nice. Then... you'll never know what happened next... this lady zoomed me with another noisy thing and I saw my lovely curls falling all over the place. I looked at mommy in horror and squeaked a bit, but she just smiled and said "It's OK, Mitch" over and over. When it was done and I was dried, this lady brushed me... I liked that a lot. I felt light and free without all those curls... and I could see without all the fuzz in front of my eyes. It was worth all that hullaballoo though because the razor lady and my mom just oooh-ed and aaahed all over me... I got a Milkbone treat and cuddles before I left the hairdresser place and my mom just kept looking at me as if she didn't know me anymore. "Where's my little brown bear gone?" she kept wailing. Well, she's wrong. My bear is blue and is at home in my bedroom crate having his afternoon nap. The lady said "See you again, Mitch. You have been an angel". What's an angel? Can I eat it? Or does it squeak when I play bite it? So many new things every day.

Well, naptime. See ya!

Yip!

Zzzzzzz.

I got my new food dish and my own dining area

This is so much fun...come play, dad!

Here I am taking my dad for a walk. I love walkies!

mitchell

FEBRUARY 22

It has been 4 weeks now that I've lived here... and so much has been happening. I am so pleased to say that I am doing a good job with my new people! I can get them to give me a treat just by peeing outside! I can get them to give me a Milkbone just by running to my bed when they say, "Mitch, crate!" They do little dances, and I get tickles when I sit or come to them when they call my name... it was so easy to train them to do that!

I have sniffed every corner of the house and know every place I can hide my toys. Funny though, whenever I do hide a toy it walks away when I am not looking... but I find it in my toy box! Some toys are very squeaky, some bouncy, and some chewy. I like my soft squeaky ones best! My blue bear is my bestest toy, and he sleeps with me in my bed.

I have been for walkies with my new green jacket on. Yesterday I went to a place called a bank. I had to stand with my Mom behind other two-legged giants and then sit (Mom pushes my hiney down with her finger so I know what to do), then I moved forward, then had to sit again, and do it over a few times until we got to this high wall. I could not see over, but a face peeped over the top and when I looked up, a person said "Hi, Mitch! Welcome to our bank!"

I was ooohed and aaahed at many times. I like that! They say I am doing well... no idea what that means! I have been to my people's friends' houses to visit. This is new to me and I am a bit shy at first... but everyone is talking to me and telling me I am such a good boy. How come Mom doesn't let them give me tasty morsel treats?? They eat some themselves! No fair! Mom takes me outside if I nap for a bit... and we go through that game where when I pee I get a treat and watch their silly dance!

Did I mention snow before? This is soooo neat! I can bury my head in this cold white stuff and hide. Mom or dad call me and I pretend I can't hear them. Then when they move away to look for me somewhere else, I pop out and chase them. It is easy to make them laugh. I shake my body and the wet snow flies all over their feet and they jump around trying to escape me! I love snow!

One visit wasn't so much fun... I went to someone called vet and she stuck 2 needles into my hiney! I will pee on her table next time! Best of all, I went to this big noisy place with lots of people who were eating something called chocolate and there was music. It smelled delicious! Mom picked me up and carried me around cause I got a little wimpy looking up at all those long legs. I was NOT SCARED... well just a little, maybe.

I wanted to see faces, because they come close enough to lick sometimes... and people talk to me in this high squeaky voice. I don't know why, but it seems to make them happy, so I wiggle and lick, wiggle and lick. I couldn't have any treats- AGAIN! – I did hear that it was an event called "Everything Chocolate". No wonder I am so special... I'm chocolaty coloured too!

Say hello if you see me on a new adventure!!

Yip! Yip! (I am practicing my woofing... because I am getting to be bigger now and yipping is what puppies do).

I LOVE SNOW!!!!

PHOTO COURTESY OF BIJOU POODLES

Where did the ball go?

MARCH 8

Hey, Everyone... it's me... Mitch!

I bet you have been wondering how I spend my time each day. Here's a sample for you.

8.00a.m.	Food! My favourite thing!
9.30a.m.	A car ride! My favourite thing!
9.40a.m.	A walkie around the village! My favourite thing!
10.30a.m.	Belly rub and tickle from Mom! My favourite thing!
12.00p.m.	Lunch! My favourite thing!
12.30p.m.	Outside to pee and play! My favourite thing!
1.00p.m.	Afternoon nap! My favourite thing!
3.00p.m.	Play 'come' and 'sit' for treats! My favourite thing!
4.00p.m.	Lie on dad for belly rubs and paw massage! My favourite thing!
5.00p.m.	Supper! My favourite thing!

6.00p.m.	Milkbones! My favourite thing!
7.00p.m.	Play with ball! My favourite thing!
8.00p.m.	Watch TV lying on dad's feet! My favourite thing!
9.00p.m.	Off to my crate for a lovely long sleep! My favourite thing!

Not so bad, huh? Next week I am told I am going to a mall, whatever that is.

Bye for now. Wif!

(I have not got the big dog sound right yet... still practicing... but it would go faster if barking was not another no-no!)

MARCH 9

Hello! Hello! How are you? See, I am improving with my social manners. I can shake a paw, and I sort of mostly know when to sit quietly and when it is OK to meet and greet! I don't always get it right. Sometimes it is more fun to pretend I don't know at all.

Mom and Dad have now taken me to a couple of nearby smelly food places... resto-something... where people go to eat. I know I have to go straight underneath the table and lie down. Mom says if I am a nuisance they will have to take me out and I won't get to explore all the interesting things I find under the table. I don't get human food at home... but this is a wonderful treaty kind of place... I found a French fry yesterday. Don't tell anyone. I find all kinds of new things under there.

Dad likes to take me for walkies. Well... that's what he calls it. Actually, I am the one taking him. I run ahead of him on my leash until I am pulling him along. Then he gives me a little tug and says "Heel, Mitch". That means if I trot back to him I can make him give me a treat. He is so easy to fool... so I run ahead and wait for him to think he is telling me what to do... then I pretend I care what he is saying and get a treat too! It is a really fun game.

It is time for my nap with my bear. Sometimes I can sneak another toy in there, but if it squeaks when I am supposed to be sleeping, mom comes and gets it. I think she likes to play with toys too.

Bye... night night! ZZZzzzzzzz.

mitchell

MARCH 14

Spring is here! Spring is here! I won't know where to do my business when the snow banks are gone... my people are worried about that! Don't know why. I have trained them to pick up after me anyway!

My people say I bounce like a jack rabbit too much... I like doing animal impressions... but apparently that is a no-no. So many no-no's.

This has been an exciting week! I went to the doggy beauty parlour again and the razor person was amazed at how much I have grown since my first hair cut a month ago. I don't think I eat too much, but I am training my people to give me treats. I just act confused when they give me a command. Then I get it right and they go into their silly dance thingy and I get the treat. They are so easy to fool! So I guess I am growing big.

Twice this week I have visited the 'city', walking through that mall place. Mom and Dad say it now takes them ten times as long to walk from one end of the mall to the other because of me. What did I do wrong? I am just being polite stopping to say hello to people who come to talk. I am small but mighty, my Mom says... I can draw all these people to me and keep them entertained... See? I've still got IT!

I got to ride on an escalator... well, I didn't actually volunteer. Strange. Stairs that move and disappear! Does that store know their stairs get lost? I would have fetched them but my person picked me up at the top before I could figure out where they went! It felt really funny on my feet... front paws moving up, back paws on a different step at a different level. Front paws losing the step while back paws still moving! We went round a few times until I got tired of that game. Mom put me on the steps coming out of the ground... and picked me up again at the top as the stairs went back in. Lots of people watching... I couldn't smile at them too much because those stairs kept me busy trying to figure them out.

Went to a meeting with a bunch of LIONS! I thought I'd be scared and that they might eat me. But it was OK. Not even a roar! They were people just pretending to be Lions, I think. My mom told me they were members of the Lions Club and were interested in me because they raise a lot of money so that furry people like me can be trained to become very special indeed!

My people are learning lots... and dancing when they get things right!

See ya around!

Woof! Yip! Woof! Yip!

Up and down and up and down and up and down...
think I got it!

mitchell

MARCH 22

Life continues to be exciting, scary, smelly and tasty. Each day my people introduce me to new things... some I like, others are a big yawn!

Let's see... the folk at a Home for very old people-thingies smell really interesting... I go there a lot for hugs. Mom puts me on someone's knee and I snuggle up to them and teach them to tickle and stroke me. They learned really fast! Some of them sneak teeny bits of treats to me when my Mom isn't looking.

The traffic in the city doesn't smell nice, but I am not so jumpy now. I met a bus this week. I was sitting at the curb, minding my own business, and this big thing came by and let out a big HHSSSSSS!! Sure made me move in a hurry! My people say I have to get on one of those things one of these days. NOT!

The mall is a breeze now. I'm still a little spooked when I meet a two-legged people-thingy whose eyes are the same level as mine. What are they? Their fingers taste good though!

You should see me on the disappearing stairs now... way cool! I can step on by myself... look around as I travel upwards... and when my mom says "Mitch, jump!" I make a big leap to solid ground. I always look around to see if my audience saw me fly through the air!! They are grinnin' fools... like me. My mom calls me that. It is her pet name for me.

St. Patrick's day was way cool, too. It was my 5-month birthday and I wore my best green outfit and went to Irish Stew Day on my Island. Lots of people and gooood smells! Then, because I was being very good that day, we went on to the Legion to get wings, or something. I didn't learn to fly though... so confusing! There was a herd of those little people thingies there... hmmm. Not sure if I should play with them, eat them, or drag them around the room and get them to chase me! One was the size of my teddy bear, but it wasn't blue.

One place I know well now is Auntie Gloria's office... always get good treats there...the best! And I met something Dad called a puppy. Hah! I know a puppy when I see one. I am a puppy. This little thing was tiny and squirmy! Can't fool me. This was a um...morsel!

Woof! Yip! Woof!

Me and my dad playfighting.......we boys like to playfight!

Ohhh...I love a head rub!   Aaaah... I love a body rub

MARCH 29

Hi, Everyone!

I have good news... and bad news! The good news is I'm in love... I'M IN LOVE... I'M IN LOVE! Saturday evening after a busy, exhausting day in the city (Yep, they got me on a BUS! I'll tell you more about that later), I was going for a nice calm walkie with my Mom person. Suddenly, I had this creepy feeling and when I looked over my shoulder, there, walking quite far behind me with her people parents, was this golden four-legged beauty! Wow! I was so desperate to meet her, so my mom waited as this gorgeous creature came up to me and I could meet her, nose to butt. Then she was whisked away and my mom had to hold me very tight as I was determined not to let Goldie out of my sight!

The bad news is... I was out of my mind for the rest of the evening...crazy, my dad says! Running in circles round the house... yipping and yapping like never before! Doggone it, what's a fella to dooooo? Wherefore art thou, sweet smelling delight?

Woof! Woof! (those are REAL woofs now for some reason!)

P.S. What does 'neutering' mean?

Here's the card I got in the mail... first ever love letter!

APRIL 4

Oh, Boy! I had quite a week!

The good news today is that Spring really is here! I have found out what I am supposed to do with my business now that the snow is all gone. Seems that grass is an acceptable toilet for me. And my people are happy as it is easier for them to pick up after me (Yes, I still have the power to make them clean up after me!)

Speaking of grass... I've been eating it. Don't know why. Makes me sick. You should see my people leap up and pay attention when they hear me heaving behind the couch!! FUN!

The bad news is... burrs! I found out the hard way that when you roll in them you have to go and get a haircut. That razor lady again! I'm NAKED!

Burrrrr... Brrrrr... Grrrrr!

I think I will spend the rest of my life in my bedroom. *Don't look at me!!*

Cheap toy, dad!

mitchell

APRIL 12

Hi, y'all!

My beloved snow is back! How I love playing in it... eating it... and helping my dad shovel it!He takes a shovel full and throws it in the air... and I jump high and bite it. So much FUN!

My curls are growing back again after my last skirmish with the razor lady! Most people don't know I am a standard poodle because I don't look very "poodle-y"... no pom-poms or top-knots. Dad is happy about that as he says no male dog should be made to parade around with a frou-frou haircut! I so agree! Men understand these things.

I met a lot of people at the Maple Sugar Festival...lots of oooohing and aaaahing and, "Hi, Mitchell." (Everybody knows me... I am famous!) This island home of mine is very famous for its maple syrup...they don't *make* it, they *catch* the liquid running from a tree, and then they cook it. Sounds odd to me. Did you know that trees pee?

Last week I attended a class at the high school where I had to behave and sit nice-nice for ages. Dad was talking to a class there about the Lions Clubs and an upcoming fundraiser called the Purina Walk for Dog Guides. I will be leading that walk. I am the St. Joseph Island Lions Club's mascot!! I am sooo excited! Mom says I must be very, very good... and I may get to meet some other dogs! (Goldie????)

See ya!

Mitch

Snowing again! YAY!

APRIL 26

Hi, it's me, Mitchell

What a busy time I have been having! I went with my two-legged parents to the Lions Club's pet cemetery on 'P' Street (P? get it? Heeheehee). My mom and dad told me they help people bury their pets when they die (what is that?) and the club gets a little more money to buy and train guide dogs. (Do they dig 'em up like I do with my buried bones?) Anyhoo, we went there to rake a million leaves from last Fall. Want to hear Lions roar? Dive bomb a pile of leaves they have just spent ages raking!

I didn't know that the money raised by the cemetery and the bridge walk help to buy guide dogs like me... they tell me I am expensive and cost thousands of dollars in my life time. I AM made of gold and chocolate!!

I am finally an expert at bus rides. I am enjoying it now that I can sit on my Mom's knee and see out the window. At first I could not get up the big step, then I had to walk up a path between chairs to find one that mom wanted.

I don't get to choose who I sit next to, apparently. Mom wants to sit near the front...and I want to go to the back. Why can't I? I can go by myself, but she won't let me. Pfft!

I see trees and houses and people whizzing by. At first I thought I was supposed to chase and fetch... but mom held on to me too tightly, so I couldn't. I can't say I like the smells on a bus, and Mom says soon I will have to learn to sit on the floor at her feet. That will be good because I see hidden treats stuck to that floor, which I, and I alone, will eat! And she won't know. Ha!

**Love my toy with peanut butter inside it...
takes me AGES to lick it out!**

I pulled my pad out so I can see you …
I like to keep my eyes on you...

mitchell

MAY 10

Hello!

Did you miss me last week? I was off on an adventure with my Mom and Dad. It was my 6 month check-up at the Lion's Foundation in Oakville, where I come from, far away from my Island home. It is where the big training school is for us special dogs like I will be one day. Imagine my delight when we got there and there was a posse of pups! Mom says there were over 25, with their people. It was a bit noisy and we all tried to meet each other at the same time. So many butts – so little time!

Some were tiny (dad says Jack Russell terriers, who might be 'hearing assistants' one day) and there were oodles of poodles just like me. There were a lot of labs, and there was one white standard poodle and a bunch of brown ones like me. One was my sister, but she didn't recognize me. However, I was the tallest and the finest of them all! Just ask dad. Must be the wonderful St. Joseph Island air!

We went for a long walk all in a row through the downtown, and then we had to climb up and down these scary stairs called fire escapes. Some couldn't do it... BUT I DID IT! Then we went for coffee at Timmy Somebody's. Well, Mom and Dad and all the other moms and dads did. We had to go in with them to show manners, though. I made my parents proud, they said. Not perfect, but nearly. The big boss trainers seemed to like me too, so I guess I passed the test this time! So happy to be home again!

Licky kisses from Mitch!

mitchell

MAY 3

It's me, Mitchell, woofing!

I love walkies. The more walkies the better. I drag my dad out on walkies whenever I can. Walkies are good. So... imagine my delight when the Lions Club asked me to be the lead walkie person for this Bridge Walkie thingy coming up soon! Yippee! It's like taking aMilkbone from a puppy! For the occasion I am getting a new Future Dog Guide coat because I am too big for my puppy one, a new collar and leash (purple, the Lions Club colour, (... and my favourite colour, remember?), and... a haircut (BOO!). It will be *me* guiding everybody... I hope you will be proud of me! Mom says I have to get used to 'leading', as I will be going to Doggie University when I am a bit older to learn how to really be a guiding dog. I hope it doesn't hurt.

I practice my walking more now... there is a lot of sitting required too. Walk, stop, sit... walk some more, stop, sit... wish my peeps would make up their minds! Dad takes me out to a safe place and we practice something called sit/stay. He tells me to sit and I do... then he tells me 'stay' and waves his hand in front of my nose. Then he walks away from me. It was hard not to run after him at first, but I am good now... I know he will turn around and call my name... and then I let him give me a treat when I run up to him.

Woofingly yours,

Mitch...

relaxing!

mitchell

MAY 25

HEY!

I have learned two new very useful tricks. Both show how much smarter four-legged critters are than the two-legged kind. First, you know I am not supposed to eat "human" food (who eats humans anyway?). Well, if my mom is eating ice cream, I become all lovey-dovey, put my head on her arm or knee, look up at her adoringly with just a little of the whites of my eyes showing, bat my long eyelashes and let out the teeniest whimper ...and I get a bit of the treat, if there is nobody looking!

Second, I am only allowed to play with my own toys which are kept in my toy box. So, if there is something of 'theirs' I want, (like a sock or underpants) I take it when they are not looking and put it in my toy box, next to my other teddy bear and under my chewy stuff. Later on, when they say "go get a toy", I trot over to my toy box and get my 'new' toy. Fair game, right? Well... you'd think so... not quite perfected that one yet, but I am working on it!

See you next week at the Bridge Walk for Dog Guides!!

Your friend, Mitch

Mommee... pretty please... just a little bit...... pleeeze!

mitchell

JUNE 14

The Bridge Walkie was AWESOME! I walked at the head of this long line of two-legged critters... some with four-legged friends attached, many just on their own. Nobody got lost or fell off the Bridge... because I did so well! I was so admired! I really caught the eye of a beautiful lady dog too ...silky coat... come-to-crate eyes! I managed to get a little smoochin before we were cruelly separated. What is unrequited love? Mom says my head swelled up twice the size... I have no idea what that means... my head feels normal to me. I have a very nice head!

The only person wearing a Persian lamb fur coat, though, was me. Hot! Good job there were lots of bowls of water along the route. I believe I am the best future dog guide there is... everyone says so.

Me, leading the Purina Walk for Dog Guides over the
St. Joseph Island Bridge

On Sunday I took my people to the city for a Music Festival called Beer, Bratwurst and Beethoven. Well, for me it was Water, Milkbones and Noise! It was fun though. I walked around so nicely. I met babies in buggies and licked their very tasty little fingers! I met a few other dogs, nose-to-nose (no butts allowed). No chemistry, though... or should I say biology? (Goldie?....oh, sorry, pardon, wrong again). Mom took a few videos of me to send to Lions Foundation so they could check my progress... cheaper than a trip to Oakville, dad says... but not as much fun, I say!

What's a goofball? Apparently, I am one of those too. Is it anything like stud muffin? That's hopeful!

See you next week... Mitch

Strutting my stuff – look how good I do it!

My friends are LIONS...but they don't bite!

Me and my dad leading the pack on a
Purina Walk for Dog Guides!

JUNE 21

Guess what! I'm getting fan mail!!!

Remember I told you last week about that lovely silky black and white pooch I met at the Bridge Walk... the one I smooched with? Well, I got a letter from her... ahem!.... HIM. Talk about feeling foolish... I'm not sure what it means when I don't know a boy from a girl dog. Mom says it's because I am only allowed to sniff face... not... elsewhere. Ah, well... anyhoo... it was nice to get a letter. It was from Casey, a Cavalier King Charles Spaniel. That sounds a bit posh to me. I wish I was a Knight King Mitchell Poodle. I am not worthy! I am not worthy!

Sooo looking forward to seeing HIM again!

Woof

Lord Mitchell of St. Joseph Island
(just kidding, Casey!)

DEAR MITCHELL
I saw you at the
Walk. I followed you
all the way over the
bridge. It was a
lot of fun.
I would like to be your
friend. I saw you
looking at me so I know
you like me too.
I will share my treats
with you.   CASE

The second letter I ever got! Wow! I got mail!

mitchell

JUNE 28

Yikes... it sure gets hot around here! And I am not allowed to go to the beach to swim. Something about... if I am leading a blind person, and I'm hot, and I see a lake...?

My favourite place is the pet cemetery up on "P" street...(P? teehee!). I love to run around there in the shade of the trees, and sniff at the granite markers of the pets who live there now. I like to chase the earth as dad digs it up and throws it... it is nice and cool. When there is a pile of earth I like to surprise my dad and jump in it... and practice my digging skills. I do not know why he yells when I am doing that. Perhaps because he wanted the pile all for himself? Selfish...or what? But he doesn't yell half as loud as Mom does when we come home from digging practice and I run into the house to find her! Has my name changed to "OUT" or what?

Stay cool, fellow earthlings!!

I can guard the door and stop drafts all at
the same time!

JULY 12

I have met so many nice people lately and everybody says "Hello, Mitch!" I am sooo famous! My Mom says she feels like chopped liver. I don't get that! When I lick her she tastes of salt, pineapple sunscreen, dish detergent, or whatever... never liver! She's nuts! (Oh, that's why she tastes salty!).

You should see me walking figure eights now. I bet you don't know what that is! When we are practicing my 'walking to heel', dad will walk around in what he calls figure 8 and I have to pay very close attention so I don't get knocked with his knee or stepped on. So, I watch him carefully and try to sense when he is going to do a tricky move so I can stick close by his left leg and match his direction. Apparently, that is a very advanced move... and he, therefore, is a very advanced trainee!! It is really fun, because dad keeps trying to trick me and head off in another direction really fast... but I win every time, because I can feel in my bones when he is going to make a move.

I am not getting treats every time I guess what they want me to do anymore... just sometimes. But I never know when that sometimes will be, so it is a surprise.

Woof! Woof! (did you hear that? Mom says my voice has broken, but I didn't do it! Honest!)

Mitch

I go to work with mommy... booooring!

Letting teddy rest a little before we wrestle some more!

JULY 26

Help! Help me! There are little creatures running around on two legs in my house... there are wet towels and there is sand everywhere... and it is NOT my fault.

But let me start from the beginning. We went on this loooong car ride to get these... alien creatures. I don't see what's so 'grand' about them! There are three of them! Yep, I'm outnumbered. One has long black hair which I like to pull. She squeaks when I do, and I don't know if she is a puppy, a squeaky toy, or what. She cuddles and plays with me, so she is growing on me daily. I get into trouble when I try to crawl into bed with her though.

We also have another girl creature whom I know well... she used to be scared of me but now knows I am an OK guy. She makes me sit and stuff, but I like the way she tickles my feet.

The other is Mr. Cool... and he and his friend catch FROGS and other things. Mom isn't too thrilled about that, I can tell you. If I brought home the skull of a mouse thingy like these creatures do... I'd be dead meat! So NOT fair!

Ah, well... it's a dog's life!

Your befuddled friend,

Mitch

Licky kisses For my friend

mitchell

AUGUST 9

This is the last week for the two-legged critters who have been littering my house. It will be very nice to have my space back... and my Mom and Dad's undivided attention! But I will miss them. Apparently, this was a big test for me... not being used to young people pups. Mom said I was a bit rambo--something with the kids...no idea what that means. Probably something to do with the fact that they always taste so good, so I chase them to lick them! And their toys are better than mine!

Next, my dad says, I have to learn to play with dogs. I get so excited when I see one that I forget my manners. I have to get used to being with them, so I can ignore them. That doesn't make a lick of sense to me! Anyhoo... we now have a big fence round our yard... and dad says I can invite four-legged friends over with their parents. So, is there anyone out there interested? I'm a big nine month old rough puppy. Casey... OK? And maybe Molly?...and what about those lovely Airedales we saw? They are my

size and might put me in my place, mom says! What...?
    Call my parents to apply for the job!
    See ya
    Wuffers

I wuff my dad

AUGUST 23

My... how quiet it is around here! Those 2-legged little people critters are gone. We went on a long car ride again and put them on this big bird thing which took them up into the sky. I really miss them! Especially the smallest one as she let me sneak into her bed when mom and dad weren't looking. She didn't make me sit for a treat... she just went to the magic drawer and gave me a handful whenever she wanted. I really liked her. Dad says my training has gone to somewhere up a hill in a hand basket! I keep going to the door of the little room where I can still smell them... but they are really gone! I feel a bit mopey now... so boring without them!! They were so close to the floor that we could roll around and tickle each other.

Mom said to thank all the people who were so kind to them... lending toys and games... and videos for our visitors. I liked Mr. Bean. Mom has a photo of me and the little one lying on her bed watching that video... hmmm, evidence NOT to be shared with Lions Foundation! Dog on bed? NOT!

While they were here, dad did take me to the beach and I got to go in the water. Everyone was laughing at me... something to do with me being a jack rabbit again.

Next adventure... getting to meet a four-legged friend called Fergus the Airedale. I must not get too excited! I must not get too excited! Right? Right. Next time I'll tell you how it went.

What does "dog days of summer" mean?

Wuff you lots!!

AUGUST 30

Hey!

Last time I wrote to you I was going to have a play date with Fergus. (He also has 4 legs!). Well, it happened and we got along famously. He plays as hard as I do... he slobbers more than I do and globbed all over me (but I didn't mind)... and he gets almost as excited as I do. We galloped, rolled and hurtled around the yard for an hour or so. I was so pooped out that my tongue hung almost to the ground. And I panted and panted. It was so much fun! We were so fast that we could sniff butt on the run with nobody's mom noticing!

Afterwards, I had to endure a bath with smelly bubbly stuff so I wouldn't offend the delicate noses of my people! Spoil sports... don't they know that smell is essential to a dog's self-esteem? We even leave p-mail whenever we are out for walkies. There are some very interesting doggies around this island that I haven't even seen, but we leave all these messages for each other. I may not know these doggies personally, but I hope to meet some of them soon!

And I'll tell you something else... I am sick of being dragged to a tent thingy at a parking lot in the city to 'help' sell riffle tickets or ruffle tickets or whatever. We spent hours in the parking lot of a big store... and Mom got all the attention. People would come over to us when they saw me in my purple Lions Club Mascot jacket... but that mean ol' Dad would divert their attention from me to her... and they would laugh and smile with Mom... and buy a riffle ticket, or something like that! I just don't get it. I couldn't even eat the ticket. Grrrrr... ppfft.

Nobody wuffs me... ☹

The colour of the water shows what a good time I have been having!

Are you talking to me??

Helping my dad. He couldn't do it without me! I am learning to be a good helper... remember... I am a future doggy assistant!

mitchell

SEPTEMBER 6

Phew! No more selling tickets... am I happy it is all over and done with? You bet your bippy I am! Now attention will once more be riveted on me all the time... where it should be!

Actually, the best part of this whole thing, when I went to the big store with my Dad and Mom, was when they walked me up and down in front of that ticket selling table. Being the 'chick' magnet that I am, I drew a lot of attention and people came closer so Mom and Dad and the other Lions could catch them. (It was like fishing, I'm told... with me as bait!). It was lovely being fussed over and treated like the Prince that I am! I would sit and pose... or walk and preen myself! Dad said I earned my keep that week. I don't know what that means exactly... anyhow, I liked it. Because of me, the Lions Club made a lot of money for dog guides. Yay for me!!

The next thing on my list is meeting other dogs, playing with other dogs... and something called 'snip snip'... that sounds like fun!

What's around the next corner I wonder??

Wuff

I came to work with mom today and now I'm tired...

Pulled my mat in front of the fireplace...
keeping an eye on things.

I love my dad ☺

SEPTEMBER 13

All today my mom has been whispering "Snip, snip" in my ear! What's with her? When she was saying that last week I thought it was because I was going to have a haircut... but that happened on Saturday... and it was more of a "Buzz, buzz"... and now I am NAKED again! Hide me! *Don't answer the door!*

SEPTEMBER 14

Everyone was up early this morning... joy, oh joy! But I was hungry. Won't somebody FEED me, please, I kept signaling my "I'm hungry" signal... Nobody listened. Then Dad and I went on an early car ride...my favourite thing!

LATER
SEPTEMBER 14

I am not speaking to anybody ever again. That early car ride was a TRICK! Dad took me to that place of the needles... and... well, it is unspeakable what they did. I'm feeling very weird. And there's a space where my you-know-what was you-know-where. I'm curled up in my safe place... not playing... not plaaaaaying... not plaaaaa... zzzzzzzz.

NEXT DAY

Finally... SOMEONE is feeding me... and I'm getting treats and back rubs. Mom is hugging me. Dad is saying "Sorry, Buddy" over and over again! What's with these people... I'll get my ball and we'll play catch to cheer them up. Did someone say ball?

mitchell

SEPTEMBER 20

Hi, it's me! What's left of me anyway! Really, I am feeling just fine... thanks for all the Get Well cards! There was an article in our local newspaper, with a Tweety Bird in it wishing me well... how cool is that? And, I got Dad's nose out of joint when I told him to go to the lady of the needles and have her do to him what she did to me, so he can enjoy all the tummy rubs and back rubs from Mom, and to get cards from people, too. Funny, though, he just turned white and went to lie down.

Anyway, I have to buckle down now and stop goofing around. So it's "stay," "sit," "down," "come," "stay,"....over and over! We are practicing, Mom says, for a test coming up in two weeks at the puppy place. I'm nervous and excited. So much so that I bounced high in the air and gave dad a black eye on Monday. But when you see him, pretend you don't believe him when he tells you how it happened. Just ask him if Mom's knuckles are getting better! I dare ya!

OK... I'm sitting already! ☺

Look...more mail!

Some of my two-legged fans! Aren't I handsome?

Notice my brown nose. I'm told this is very classy!

Me and my toy box – I like to nap here instead of my crate. Sometimes it's a good hiding place, too, for mom and dad's underwear when I take them!

mitchell

OCTOBER 4

Hello, everybody!

I just got back from a long, long drive. Dad kept telling me I was going to checkout my new home... no idea what he's mumbling about. There's this big place I've seen over the last few days. It's big, with lots of 2-legged creatures who all smell like dogs. It's wonderful!! They smell like that because there are a lot of 4-legged critters around, more of *them* than the 2-legged kind. What kind of Paradise is that? There are lots of little tiny creatures, some that look like me only smaller... black shiny ones, and long golden haired ones (Goldie, is that you?)... and curly coated ones. They are all wearing little coats like mine, only some are different colours. Most have 2-legged creatures attached to them, and all have the waggiest tails and the laughiest grins! We all had to parade around and do those figure eights, the sit/stay game, and the come-when-called trick. I wanted to look around to see everybody strut their stuff, but mom kept tugging my head around so I focused on my 'work'. Work? This is FUN.

Everywhere I looked there were crates with toys and blankies. I can tell these are sleep places. I have one at home, and I really like mine and hide in it whenever I want some peace and quiet... or just 'space', as Mom keeps whining about. Lots of 2-leggers made a big fuss over me and kept saying "See you soon, Mitch". I guess I will be going there again... hope they let me play with some of those toys sometime!

Wuffs to everyone!!

Your friend, Mitch

mitchell

OCTOBER 25

It's me, Mitch

I'm a bit confused these days. My routine seems to have gone all to pot! I can't find my dad anywhere...I've looked under the beds and in the cupboards and behind the shed, but he has got a really great hiding place this time. And my mom is gone a lot these days too. I hope she's shopping for treats for me!

On the other paw, my house has a bunch of two-legged visitors who play with me lots... and I hear them laughing their heads off at me when I act goofy. During the day I have to be a good boy and stay in my crate more than usual... and then Auntie Bonnie Puddingstone or Auntie Mary Kay come over and play with me outside... boy! They need some lessons on soccer! I love it when someone new comes to play with me because I can trick them into throwing the ball so many times they are pooped!

Some big surprise is being planned for me. I can feel it in my bones. I see Mom looking at me and talking in that ear thingy... something about crates and planes and training... I think I am going on a trip soon. Yippee!!

I don't know where my daddy is... he's still hiding and mom is using up lots of those tissue things which I love to steal out of the bathroom trash bin! Do I ever get into trouble for that! Ah, well... still a lot of no-no's.

Your faithful friend the frenzied fuzzy-faced Mitch

I miss my daddy!

I'm too big for my crate now – but I still love it!

Don't bug me... it is nap time!!

NOVEMBER 10

Postcard from Mitch

I'm sure you are wondering where I am! Well, here I am. I know Mom put me in a strange box and put me in this big bird-like thingy. I know this really nice two-legged creature helped me escape from this box a while later and gave me treats and walkies, and I rode in his car to this new place. But... folks!....this is Heaven! There are other four-legged peeps everywhere for me to play with... and two-legged creatures who talk to me, play with me, and give me treats for being a good boy. A new mommy... again. Nice one!

I am *trying* to be a good boy! Mom whispered in my ear that I was to try not to be so goofy... and to close my mouth if I can't help jumping around in case I bite my tongue... REALLY? That was the last thing she said before giving me a hug and a kiss and saying "Goodbye, Mitchell. You're the best!" I don't know why she didn't come with me this time. Or why Dad wasn't there.

The other day I had a white-coat check me all over my body. I thought it was another 'needle' person...but no. This white coat gave me a sort of body rub...but not as good as my Mom used to give me. Elbows and hips... elbows and hips, she kept muttering. What does that mean? Maybe because I am so clumsy she didn't think I knew my elbows from my hips?

Anyhow... I'm being watched all the time, so I am REALLY trying to make a good impression. Don't know what's next. I'll send you a postcard every once in a while to let you know all about my new adventure.

Miss you, Mom and Dad... but not all that much. Life is grand and busy and fun!

Love, Your goofy boy, Mitch

DECEMBER 6

Postcard from Mitch

Hey, Everyone! Here I am in that big, busy, smelly place... doggie university?I stayed in that first place for a few weeks, and then I was brought here. I've been poked and prodded, x-rayed and weighed. I've seen a dentist, a vet, had my eyes checked, and my hearing too. They say I have two good eyes and two good ears, all my joints are strong and my bones straight... all that hard work and my mom could have just told them if they'd asked!

Different trainers have walked me, played with me, and taught me stuff... I've walked beside wheelchairs, up and down escalators (I'm really good at that), on and off buses... and all they say is "He's such a happy boy!" Dad had asked them what they meant by that and was told "He's so rambo-something!" Where have I heard that before? Now I know it means rambunctious which I know is a good thing... right?

Oh, boy! Mom told me to calm down. On the other hand, I'm still young, they keep saying, so as time passes I'll find my calm place. Is that different from my happy place?... because someone should tell them I have found that!

I have lots of friends and am having a terrific time... so I'll send you another postcard at a later date.

Miss you, St. Joe Island and all my fans!

mitchell

DECEMBER 20

A Postcard from Mitch

I get messages all the time from my Dad and Mom on St. Joseph Island... and Dad says that people don't seem to be asking how HE is... you just ask about ME!! So, let me give you a bit of an update...

Based on the games I like to play, it has been decided that I will fit into the Vision program. There are 6 programs and me and my doggie friends are now slowly being divided among those programs, depending on how we play, what we like to do, and how strong we are. My new teacher's name is Courtney, and I am learning to walk into my harness on command, to walk better at heel and...to refuse food. What? You say... refuse food? Yep. You heard right. I'm only supposed to eat from my own bowl and only from my person. I can never take treats from anyone else or eat something found under a table!!

It's challenging, but I am trying very hard... there's a long way to go, they say, but if I can learn everything well, I should be graduating in a few months. It does take a long time to train a real dog guide at a real doggie university.

I'll try to write you again when I know some more stuff... but I am sooo busy, you will have to forgive me if I just don't have time!

Wuff! Wuff! Wuff! (in case you can't hear my bark, it is now deep and quite loud.)

mitchell

MAY OF THE NEXT YEAR

Postcard from Mitch

I have had a very good few months learning and learning and learning... and I love learning new things and then practicing until I am the best I can be!

These two-legged critters here know how to treat a guy and how to make work out of a game,(as they say).

I have now met my new forever person. He is a visually impaired tall guy who likes to be active... and I, yes, **me**... I am going to be his guide so he can enjoy his life. I am so proud! I *graduated*!! ☺

I saw you, Mom and Dad, at my graduation yesterday. It was the first time you had seen me in 6 months. I knew you right away but I couldn't say 'hi' then because I was working when I walked onto the stage with the other graduating dogs and our new forever people! So glad I got to give you each a kiss later when we met after the ceremony, and after our harnesses had been removed. Wasn't it grand? Sorry if I almost knocked you over, Dad! I was just so happy to see you again!

There were about 12 of us dogs and our peeps graduating from the Vision program. I had spent almost a month bonding and learning with my new person, spending 24 hours a day with him here at the Doggie University. We loved each other right away!! He gives great belly rubs! You never have to worry about me... I will be A-OK!

Thank you for loving me and giving me the BEST first year a dog guide could ever have! Everything else grew from that. I loved meeting you all and knowing how much you support dogs like me and my other graduating friends. I will always love LIONS clubs because they really do live up to their motto "We Serve".

St. Joseph Island has a motto: "It takes a village to raise a child" ... or something like that. In my case, the whole Island helped raise me to be the best dog guide I could be.

Thank you, everybody. I wuff you all!!

MITCHELL

PHOTO COURTESY OF DONNA SCHELL AND PUBLISHED IN
THE ISLAND CLIPPINGS

mitchell

EPILOGUE

The Lions Foundation has recently graduated its 2000th dog guide team. This team was a Seizure Alert dog and his person. There are now six programs in which dogs can be trained, according to their natural skills and interests. They are:

- Canine Vision Dog Guide
- Hearing Ear Dog Guide
- Seizure Alert Dog Guide
- Special Skills Dog Guide (medical/wheelchair)
- Autism Assistance Dog Guide (for children with autism)
- Diabetes Alert Dog Guide (Diabetics with hypoglycemic unawareness)

This Canadian organization receives no government funding and relies on donations to provide a trained dog at NO COSTto clients. Dogs stay with their person until retirement when the dog is adopted, either by extended family or by someone from the long waiting list of people wanting to adopt an older dog from the Lions Foundation. The human half of that team can then apply for another dog guide, as they may not have more than one dog at a time. There are other accredited Dog Guide Training Centres in Canada and the U.S.A. A very similar experience during a dog's first year to Mitchell's is common. Other organizations may train dogs for people with similar disabilities, as well as P.T.S.D. and for other mental health disorders.

These graduating dogs are highly trained dog guides and are registered as such. They are not simply therapy dogs, although their therapeutic value cannot be denied.

A percentage of the proceeds from this little book will be donated to the Lions Foundation.

www.dogguides.com

FINALLY...

One last peek at some adorable puppies who are growing and learning and turning into dog guides with the love and support of foster families

ACKNOWLEDGEMENTS

- I would like to acknowledge the following for allowing me to use photographs of some of their gorgeous dogs and newborn pups:
  BIJOU Poodles,
  Contact us: brownpoodles@yahoo.com, www. bijoupoodles.com
- *I would like to acknowledge* **Erin Scott-Brown** *who designed a fabulous t-shirt for a reunion of Graduates from the Lions Foundation Dog Guides Program. She very kindly let me use the design for the cover of this book. I think it is awesome! Erin is the human half of an H.E.D. team, with her partner Fiona, a trained Hearing Ear Dog.*
- Thank you to **Donna Schell of Richards Landing**, a professional photographer for her great photo of Mitchell at 9 months all dressed up as the St. Joseph Island Lions Club Honorary Member and Mascot.

- *I am very grateful to* **Brian Fox, publisher of The Island Clippings,** *the weekly newspaper of St. Joseph Island, Ontario, for authorising my use of some material for this book. Some of it had been previously published in a little column I wrote for the Clippings when Mitchell lived there.*

- Kudos to **The St. Joseph Island Lions Club** for being so supportive of the Lions Foundation, a commitment 'To Serve' as "Knights of the Blind" as requested of Lions International in 1925 by Helen Keller.

- *I must acknowledge the fabulous army of* **foster families** *who take a pup, raise him for a year, and give him back... and sob all the way home. And they do it time after time. It has to be one of the most unselfish things anyone can do. You are my heroes!*

- And, last but not least, **Robert James Kerr, my husband,** the best doggie daddy in the world. He took all the middle of the night trips outdoors so Mitchell could be toilet trained and stay dry in his bed... he did the lion's share of the walkies... and he LOVED that darn dog!!

SUSAN M. KERR

A self-acknowledged obsessive dog lover, Sue is a Spring, Summer and Fall Northern Ontario Canadian... and a Winter Texan, spending a few months snow-free in San Benito in the Rio Grande Valley. She and hubby, Robert, are active Lions Club members, proud of the work and influence of the largest service organization in the world! Any Lions Club's first loyalty is to doing whatever needs to be done to save, preserve and enhance vision, at home and internationally. They were exhorted at an International Lions Convention in Cedar Point, Ohio in 1925 by none other than Helen Keller to "become Knights of the Blind". Canadian Lions Clubs started the Lions Foundation in 1983 and from that was born the current wonderful Dog Guide Training Centre in Oakville, Ontario, Canada, which bears the Lions name. The Centre is open for guided tours, by appointment, should you be in the Oakville area. It is in the Toronto area.

Sue is supportive of Dog and Cat Rescue organizations too, doing whatever she can to help find forever homes for abandoned and homeless animals living in shelters. She asks that you, dear reader, consider becoming a foster parent for a shelter near you. There won't be anything you do that could be more rewarding than to see your foster pet get healthy and confident, and to see it meet a new family who want to give it a permanent loving home... leaving room in your home and your heart for another desperately needy dog or cat.

SUE WITH CURRENT FOUR-LEGGED CHILD, KEISHA, AGED 7, A STANDARD POODLE. KEISHA CAME FROM LIONS FOUNDATION AFTER BEING DISQUALIFIED FROM HER TRAINING DUE TO D.A.D.D. (DOGGY ATTENTION DEFICIT DISORDER!). KEISHA ACCOMPANIES HER MOM AND DAD TO ALL FUNDRAISING SPEAKING ENGAGEMENTS ON BEHALF OF LIONS FOUNDATION DOG GUIDES.